MW01514737

PO TRIMBLE
AND THE SILVER SHREW

An episode from the Aurelian Archives
by Courtney Grace Powers

PUBLISHED BY
Courtney Grace Powers
www.aurelianarchives.com

For Trinity
Who believed in Po from the start

The Mead Moon Festival took place on the second day'a Honora's seventh full moon cluster, under the most colorful sky'a the year.

There were two kinds'a people who generally didn't enjoy the holiday as much as everyone else. Traffic control sentries, who were charged with untanglin' the influx'a horse-drawn carriages, bimotors, and automobiles, and airship mechanics, who in the weeks leadin' up to the festival were suddenly expected to take every putterin' junker with one wing in the grave and make it sky ready in time for the event.

Used to be, Po could look forward to the festival like everyone else at The Aurelian Academy. Betsy and Twill, her best friends and fellow Fourteens, had been chatterin' nonstop about it for weeks now. But this was the third year in a row the Trimble shop had been booked to capacity and then some, and Gus and Trimble just couldn't work it alone in the high season. Used to be, they didn't have to.

Po's leg bounced wildly under her wooden desk. She was tryin' to put all her anxiety into that one limb so the rest'a her could focus on what Tutor Agnes was sayin' about the hunk'a engine sittin' on a pedestal at the front'a the classroom, but it just wasn't workin'.

It was near on three o'clock. The bus-ship to Caldonia left The Owl's docks at three fifteen and didn't reach the capital city till goin' on six thirty. If she didn't bother changin' out'a her black school uniform, she could ride the trolley straight to the shop, work for three hours, and then take the bus-ship back in time for curfew. She could do her homework on the way. But would three hours be enough? Gus and Tilden couldn't afford to hire out extra help—they were strugglin' just to keep up with payin' rent on the space—but with the festival two days away and a half-dozen ships still needin' tune-ups, they were gonna be cuttin' it close. If they didn't finish on time, they couldn't take their customers' much-needed money. That was the Trimble Promise. Da had wanted them to keep it while he was away, and Po meant to make sure they did, and not just because her belly was feelin' awfully hollow these days.

She could hear the clock tickin' on the glass wall at the back'a the cube-like classroom. She fought the urge to look at it for the tenth time, playin' with her long silvery hair behind her back. When she got to the shop, she'd head straight for that Nyad Gus had been havin' trouble with. She suspected its owner had tried to fix it himself before bringin' it in, though he'd acted offended when she'd asked. But honestly, how else did an Axil-59 Eight get an outmoded connector like that in its greasers?

"Ms. Trimble," Agnes said sternly.

Jumpin', Po straightened and looked around. A few'a her classmates tittered. "Yes, Ma'am?"

Agnes eyed her flatly, one hand on the hip'a her olive jumpsuit, the other planted on the edge'a the ribbed pedestal. Her short white hair, tied back in a red handkerchief, shivered as she shook her head. Agnes *looked* grandmotherly, but she wasn't the kind'a grandma kids crossed, not unless they wanted a sore seat for the next few days.

Anges pointed her chin at the piece'a engine by her hand. "What would I need to do to have this compressor behave as an independent heat generator for its neighboring parts?"

Blinkin', Po looked closely at the piece for the first time. She relaxed as her eyes roved it, and the rest'a the class got quiet. That's what she liked best about her classes with Agnes. Everyone in here was studyin' specifically to be an airship mechanic, which meant they appreciated what they were learnin', respected it. Not like her Generally Required courses. This year, her GR was Amateur Piano. She liked playin' alright, but if she'd *really* cared about it, by this time, she would'a been two years deep in intensive classes on technique and theory. Not sittin' in the back'a the class with Twill, gigglin' when Tutor Clevenger called her playin' heavy-handed and clumsy. It was better than what he said to some people. He'd called Reece Sheppard's playin' downright *ugly* the other day.

The compressor didn't look like just a metal block to Po, but like somethin' organic that could'a been recently unearthed. The scraggly wires pokin' up from it could'a been roots. The rust in its crevices could'a been soil. She could almost smell it. It smelled like life.

"Well," she began thoughtfully, leanin' forward on her elbows, "you'd have to make sure it was good and split from the thermal generator first, elsewise you'd risk overheatin' that whole arm'a the system. In fact, I'd take the thermal generator out altogether, unless the ship in question is plannin' on breakin' orbit. From there, it's as simple as wirin' the galving links into a clean conduit to recycle the heat from nonessential systems and keepin' an eye on the undulator's R.D.A. levels."

Agnes's thin lips gathered together, wrinklin'. "Oh? Just that simple?"

The bell from the Musical Arts building sounded in the distance, and as one, her classmates rose, gatherin' up their loose leaf parchment, quills and datascopes.

"I expect your reports diagraming the full spectrum of underengine wires on my desk or in my logbox by lunch tomorrow. No excuses," Agnes called over the shuffling. She caught Po's eye as Po threw her bag over her shoulder and gestured for her to join her at her desk. With a fretful glance at the clock, Po hurried over, bobbin' anxiously from foot to foot. Agnes waited till they were alone, then sat with her hands restin' the arms'a her ladder-backed desk chair, makin' her look captainly and regal. "Ms. Trimble," she said, "this is the third day in a row you've rushed off to Caldonia like you intended to outfly a Dryad."

"It's the shop," Po explained quickly, lookin' out the window and towards the docks. They were on the other side'a The Owl's lake. She'd have to run to make it there in time. "Gus and Tilden are havin' trouble keepin' up with everythin', and my mum won't let me miss school."

Agnes nodded, unsurprised. "Still no word from your father?"

No. Not in two years, and it was like bein' punched in the heart every time she had to say so. "Not yet," she said lightly. "But you know, if he went as far as Cronus Twelve, it might be that he's still on his way back."

Or it might be that he wasn't comin' back at all. That's what Gus and Tilden believed, and what Po refused to. Believin' was easier for them than waitin' for him to return and bein' let down, and a part'a her would never forgive them for that cowardice, love them though she did. She still didn't know what Mum believed—she thought maybe she was scared to believe *anythin'*—but Po chose to think the riskier thing: that Da was still out there, lookin' for work off-world like he'd said, and that he was comin' home.

But on days like today, when there was too much work to be done and not enough hands to do it, her belief hurt especially bad.

Agnes was riflin' through the papers on her desk, lookin' for somethin'. Finally, she pulled out Po's report on fuel designations, holding it up to the light to inspect it. Po couldn't help but notice the bright red number one in its upper right-hand corner—full marks. No one ever got full marks in Agnes's class. "If you need to miss my class tomorrow," Agnes said as Po stared, "I won't dock you any points. Not when you're doing real world application of the subject matter."

"Oh! Thank you."

Agnes put down the report, looking up at her. "I've spoken very highly about you to Headmaster Eldritch, and he's taken a special interest in your talent. He would like to watch you work sometime."

Po smiled uncertainly, flattered but uneasy just the same. She didn't know any student with their head on straight who wouldn't turn around and walk the other way when they saw the headmaster glidin' towards them. Somethin' about the man was just *unsettlin'*. He reminded Po of a vulture, always circlin' campus, tryin' to find a little red meat to chew to pass the time.

"You have a gift, Po," Agnes went on, matter-o'-fact. "One I wish to see cultivated in the wild, not transplanted to some pot on a windowsill."

"Thank you," Po said again, confused. Agnes sounded like Mum, who always came down hard on Po for sayin' she just ought'a quit school and work in the shop. Mum—and Agnes, apparently—wanted her to reach her full potential. The Owl was a very nice school, and it was a wonder Po had been accepted in the first place. It would be selfish'a her to drop out when so many Westerner girls her age would never even see the campus.

She glanced out the window again and bit her lip. Uniformed students were spillin' out across The Owl's green meadows and cobbled roads. Only a few'a them would be commutin' back to Caldonia, but the bus-ship pilot wouldn't wait for nobody. "Can I—"

"Yes, yes." Agnes waved her away, returnin' to the reports scattered on her desktop. She seemed troubled. "Off with you."

Po didn't just have to run from her class to the bus-ship. She had to run from the bus-ship to the trolley, and then from the trolley to the shop. By the time she reached Western Main, she thought her back might be bruised from her bag hoppin' up and down on it.

Western Main was actually Rose Avenue, but the nickname had stuck when somewhere along the way, someone realized Rose was just a Westerner knockoff'a Main Street. The clothin' emporiums on Western Main were Westerner clothin' emporiums, with windows full'a short bustled skirts, off-the-shoulder blouses, and sleeveless wool waistcoats. The corner eateries specialized in Westerner food: potato soup, potato bread, potato crisps— hearty potato *everythin'*. Tobacco shops and apothecaries stood in for the other, more frivolous stores the real Main Street—Eastern Main—would have.

Thumbs hooked in the straps'a her bag, Po jogged up the pedestrian walkway, weavin' in and out'a the line'a black iron lampposts. Those were the same as on Eastern Main, even if the buildin's weren't. Real Main's buildin's had a lot more glass, and that made it cleaner, lighter. Here in the Mill City district, everythin' was brick and stone and covered in a thin layer'a grit, or else ash blowin' south from the factory chimneys. The air felt denser and darker, and it wasn't just a feelin'. Western Main was one thing, but the alleyways Po scurried past were deathtraps for lone shoppers. Da had always said there was no reason to be afraid'a box-dwellers, the homeless folk confined to those alleys. But he'd also said if she was walkin' home alone, he'd rather her be scared, because it would keep her smart.

She finally pulled up across the busy street from the shop, stoppin' at Bags' food cart. Bags was a boy about

Gus's age, almost old enough to graduate The Owl. He ran the cart, which was an oversized wheelbarrow with a fold out umbrella and stool, for his da, who'd lost his both legs in The Five Year Pandemic.

Bags flapped the newspaper he was pretendin' to read closed—she wasn't even sure he *could* read; a lot'a workin' Westerner kids couldn't—as she leaned against a lamppost next to him to catch her breath. He tipped back his newscap and looked out at her from under bushy brown eyebrows.

"You run here clear from Atlas?" he asked, smilin'.

"Near abouts," she panted. "And I don't think I could'a run any faster if I had a Trixt-2 Four tied to the bottoms'a my boots!"

A soft, whirring *hoot* called her attention overhead. There were three owls, small and wide-eyed, sittin' on Bags's striped umbrella. If there was one thing Western Main and Eastern Main shared, it was owls, and lots'a them. They took care'a the city's rats, but there were so many'a them leavin' their feathers and droppin's everywhere, they were practically an infestation themselves. These three were brown and tan, as tall as her forearm, with rings around their eyes. As they watched inquisitively, Po dug in the pocket'a her skirt and fished out the short stack'a crackers she had saved from lunch. She doled them out between the owls as Bags tut-tutted.

"You shouldn't feed 'em," he said, but didn't stop her. "They'll never go away, now."

"That wouldn't be so bad. You could name 'em, have 'em keep you company. Train 'em to make deliveries for you. That one," she pointed at the owl in the middle as he ruffled his wings grumpily, pushin' at the other birds, "he'd make a good watch owl. Can I name him for you? I'll name him Boxes. Then you'll be Bags and Boxes."

Shakin' his head, Bags wiggled the umbrella by its

pole, scatterin' the owls. "Po, half the time I can't tell if you're makin' fun'a me or just the strangest girl I've ever met. You gettin' the usual?"

Po flushed as he picked a warm loaf'a bread out from the belly of the barrow, already wrappin' it in brown paper. She'd had to spend her last cogs on the trolley ride. "Um, prolly not today."

Pausin' with the loaf halfway extended, Bags looked at her, then glanced over his shoulder, at the brick bakery where his mum did all the bakin'. Po tried not to look at the fresh pies steamin' up the storefront window. She could smell them from here.

"How about this," Bags suggested, smilin' after a minute. He pressed the bread into her hands as she made an objectin' sound. "I'll strike ya a deal. You take the bread on me just today, and come to the Mead Moon Festival with me day after tomorrow."

Po laughed, tryin' to shove the bread back at him, but he held up his hands, and the loaf hit his chest. "You're too old for me, Bags. Gus and Tilden would stuff you in this barrow and roll you into a grave if they thought you had intentions towards me, and then no one would get their bread on time. Besides, I can't go to the festival. I gotta help in the shop."

"All night?"

"Well…"

Bags took the loaf from her and cracked it in two with a reverent expression, lettin' steam leak out into the air. When he looked up and saw her torn look, he chuckled and wrapped the bread again. "Oh, just take it, you little urchin. I'll get you in a few years."

Thankin' him, she hurried across the street towards the shop, holdin' his gift close. Her reflection wagged on the shop window, halved by the blue and gold script readin' *Trimble and Sons* that needed touchin' up when paint could be afforded again. Through the window and the warbled reflection'a the busy street and the overcast sky behind her, she could just make out Gus standin' at their archaic monster of a cash register, a wrench clutched between his bared teeth.

The red bell on the door hinge ringed as Po slid into the shop, munchin' on her bread. She inhaled deeply. Hot metal, clean dirt, and sharp fumes greeted her familiarly.

"Ish roken again," Gus complained without lookin' at her, his fingers poised over the register's big round keys. He was so lanky, the red counter runnin' from one side'a the waitin' room to the other—to bar customers from the workshop—looked barely waist-high. Po walked up to it, frownin' at the muddy bootprints someone had tracked in on the cement floor she had just mopped last night, and it touched her bottom rib. She glanced at the tarnished silver register.

"No it ain't," she said brightly. "It's just jammed a bit. I'll fix it later."

Gus glanced at her, his white-blonde hair hangin' in his eyes. He homed in on the bread and quickly took the wrench outta his mouth. "What's that?"

"What's it look like, dummy? It's bread." Reachin' behind the counter, Po unlatched its small gate and let herself into her safe place.

A few yards behind the counter, past the stacked filin' cabinets and towerin' walls'a spare parts, the room opened up to the full width and height'a its brick exterior. It was deep and barn-like, full'a cranks and danglin' chains and two vertical translocator platforms Mr. Trimble had built himself. Three different airships were suspended at various levels in rigs'a collapsible steel nets, and the corrugated tin roof was half scrolled back on its giant gears. Gus and Tilden had prolly just sent another finished airship home.

Photon light fixtures swung lightly from metal crossbeams like vines in a Castorian jungle, blown by the tire-sized fans built into holes in the dusty wooden floors. The exposed brick walls were covered in steel lattice. It was the best way to store their tools…a hammer hooked here, a thermal torch strung up there. Plus, it was easy to climb, and it made a great coat rack in a pinch.

Po handed Gus her bread and shrugged off her bag and black jacket, then tied her hair back in a ball. Gus smelled the bread suspiciously. She smiled as his stiff expression melted into one'a silly bliss. He always worked so hard at lookin' serious, like he thought it would make him a more passable adult. There was nothin' he hated more than someone walkin' into the shop and askin' him where his parents were, or why he wasn't in school.

"Where'd you get this?" Gus asked, followin' Po back into the workshop. Overhead, the engine of an aethercopter growled rebelliously as Tilden fired it up. *Thunk, thunk.* It sounded like it had a bad leveler rod.

Po hung up her things and pulled Tilden's spare brown work shirt down off the lattice. It was identical to the one Gus was wearin', right down to its spotted black stains and wrinkles. She'd be drownin' in it, but she didn't have enough school uniforms to be flippant about gettin' this one dirty. "Bags gave it to me."

Gus gave her a look only a girl with a protective big brother would understand. He never had to say anythin' when he gave her that look, but he always did. "For what?"

She pulled on Tilden's shirt and tucked it in on the sides so it wouldn't hang to her knees. "For nothin'."

"That rat," he said vehemently, scowlin' sideways at the bread like it had betrayed him. "Now you owe him one." As the aethercopter thunked even louder, he looked up, his face smoothin' over. Mum called that the Trimble Trance. Accordin' to her, all'a her children went into it when they were lookin' at a problem needin' fixed. "Sounds like he needs to ease up on the rod," Gus murmured, bread forgotten.

Po hadn't forgotten it. She tore off a piece and stuffed it in her mouth. "He hates aethercopters, Why'd he take that one?"

Gus smiled, which was a rare site these days. In profile, he had Da's long, straight nose and one'a Mum's moon-shaped dimples at the side'a his mouth. He wasn't as handsome as Tilden, but when he smiled, he came close. "I told him I could do it faster."

They shared a devious look. In most ways, Tilden was the smartest'a them all. He was world wise and better spoken than either'a them, and that made him a good business man atop'a bein' a brilliant mechanic. But as the younger siblin's, Gus and Po liked to take each other's sides and pretend they had a special somethin' with engines that Tilden didn't. It drove him numpty. That was mostly why they did it.

After a moment, Gus's smile sank back into the worry always sittin' just beneath the surface'a his face like a bog. He looked up at the aethercopter again. "He thinks we're gonna have to close up shop, you know."

"*What*?" Po squeaked as she grabbed her favorite wrench off the wall. "No. He's just worried because we're cuttin' it so close to the festival this year."

"It ain't just that. Even if we get all the work done in time, we've been turnin' away customers we used to be able to manage. We won't make rent this month."

Po nervously gripped her wrench in both hands. She hadn't known about them turnin' away customers…that wasn't good. The more folks they turned away now, the less would try them again next month, and the month after that, until there was no one left. But they couldn't take too many on at once, or they risked not gettin' paid for their work, and that was just as bad. "I bet Mr. Barrows would give us an extension if we asked for one. Think'a all the times we've fixed that old Harpy'a his up for free!"

"He gave us an extension *last* month," Gus said, his frown deepenin' like the heavy feelin' in Po's gut. "And we still haven't been able to pay him for it." He took a bite'a bread straight off the loaf, though how he could taste anythin' was beyond Po. Her mouth felt wooden and dry.

"Mum will think'a somethin'."

Gus's look was stern as he chewed and swallowed. "No, Po. You can't tell her nothin'. You know how she is. First thing she'll do is go out and try to get some factory work that won't pay more than a couple cogs an hour, and that won't help us none. Besides. That's not what Da would want."

Gus might pretend to be angry with Da, but he was always quick to remind the lot'a them that Da might have made their family what it was, but they couldn't change just because he was gone. They could steer due north, even without him as their compass.

Po looked down at her feet. There was another option, one she was half-afraid to voice for fear this would be the time Gus finally admitted it was a good idea. Da wouldn't like it any more than he'd like the thought'a Mum leavin' life on the farm to work ten hour shifts in an assembly line, but even Po would admit he'd given up some'a his rights to fatherly disapprovals by not bein' around to voice 'em himself.

She didn't want to leave The Owl with its drippin' ivy and iron fences. She had friends there, and food, a nice room that didn't leak when the weather so much as panted. If she stayed in till she was an Eighteen and scored high enough on her career aptitude test, she could get a job on almost any ship and apprentice to the Head Mechanic until she graduated. Then she could be a real airship mechanic.

But she could be that here, too. She could help Gus and Tilden take on a full load'a customers and make their deadlines with time left to nap. The money Da had saved up for her tuition could be put back into *Trimble and Sons*, or the farm, or their bellies. Gus and Tilden, they might even be able to go out and have fun again. Date a few pretty girls. And Po, she'd be fixin' airships in one'a her favorite places in the whole world, and keepin' the shop safe until Da got back. Maybe if he got back soon, she could re-enroll at The Owl and graduate a little late. She was young for a Fourteen, anyways.

"No you don't," Tilden suddenly said. Po blinked up at him as he scrambled down a swingin' chain ladder, his tool belt rattlin'. "Gus, look at her face. You see what you've got her thinkin'?"

Gus did a short double-take, squinted at Po, and sighed. He rubbed his hair listlessly as their older brother skipped the last'a the rungs and landed beside them with a loud thump. He was shorter than Gus by half a hand, but thicker, square of shoulder and face. He used to sit on Po when she annoyed him, back before she'd figured out how ticklish he was.

"You don't know what I'm thinkin'," Po declared indignantly, hands on her hips.

"You're thinkin' about quittin' school," Tilden retorted, helpin' himself to some'a the bread. Like Gus, he looked like he hadn't seen much sunlight lately. Usually by this time'a the year, his freckles had grown so dense, his face was mottled brown. It made for a strikin' effect paired with his blue eyes. "But you wouldn't have to if you two weren't standin' around jibber-jabberin' when there's work to be done."

"But Gus says even if we finish these ships in time, it won't be enough!"

Tilden turned over his freckled arm, frownin' at a scab on his elbow. He picked at it nonchalantly. "Gus is a doomsayer. We'll be fine if everyone pulls their weight. Where'd the bread come from?"

"Bags," Gus told him darkly, and Tilden snorted, dustin' the flakes'a dried blood off his arm. Po had half a mind to wallop on them both, and the will and the wrench to do it.

The bell in the waitin' room pealed quietly.

Tilden sighed. "Somethin's numpty with the leveler rod'a that Harpy, Po."

"I got it," she said glumly. He gave her hair an encouragin' tousle as he went to man the counter and Gus started scalin' the lattice, his eyes determinedly set on the Nyad nearest the ceilin'.

Po climbed to the egg-shaped aethercopter more slowly, barely payin' attention to where she was goin' until she was suddenly sharin' the nice leather cockpit with Tilden's open toolbox. She had one brother who was careworn and somber at seventeen, and another who wanted to make her believe everythin' was right and sunny when it was more drizzly than mayday. Together, the pair would rather work themselves to bones and still lose their shop besides than let her give up the schoolin' she didn't really need.

A stubborn leveler rod was nothin' in comparison.

II

There was some kind'a commotion goin' on down on the floor.

Po frowned, pushin' open the slidin' door of the aethercopter and plantin' her boot on the wheel'a one'a its two bent, froglike legs. She leaned out into open air, her bright hair tumblin' outta its knot and hangin' over her shoulder. She could just make out Gus and Tilden between two'a the hangin' light fixtures, gesturin' emphatically as they argued. But they didn't seem angry. They seemed excited.

"What's goin' on?" she called. They ignored her. She sighed, withdrawin' into the airship to return to her work. She'd been at the aethercopter for nearly an hour. Just as soon as she checked the wear on the propeller tracks, she'd be done with her, and then she could move on to the Nyad still givin' Gus grief on the other side'a the workshop.

The propeller tracks didn't even really need checkin', but Tilden had told the pilot it could be done. The problem with busy season was that customers often brought in their ships for a tune-up and then decided they wanted new wheels and a canister change too, and all in less than a day. Po tried not to let it frustrate her. She enjoyed her time workin' more when she didn't spend it feelin' sorry for herself. Besides, most people had no idea they were bein' unreasonable, and the ones that did usually ended up takin' their business to botchy downtown mechanics who were unreasonable right back.

After hookin' a safety chain to the metal loop on her belt, Po climbed out onto the wheel and scrambled up the slanted side'a the aethercopter, which was tricky, as it had no wings. Once she reached its peak, where the leaf-shaped propellers were restin' in the off position, she snapped the goggles hangin' around her neck up onto her nose and put her face close to the rotary mast. She ran a gloved fingertip along the loops'a the propeller track, followin' the spiral down the mast. Just like she'd thought, the tracks were fine. They had a good year left before they'd need replacin'.

"Po!" Tilden called from below.

"Comin'!" Just to be thorough, Po checked the track one more time before carefully swingin' over to the lattice, where she unhooked her belt and climbed down.

Gus was pacin' circles around a floor fan, his hands steepled over his mouth like he was murmurin' secrets into them. Tilden looked up at her from a clipboard with a broad grin that made her heart twist because'a how much it resembled Da's. Their different intensities scared her a little; one looked intensely worried, and the other intensely pleased.

"Tilden? What is it? What's goin' on?"

Tilden wagged the clipboard. He'd wanted a datascope for his bookkeepin' for ages now, but he made do without. "We got a job."

"I thought we already had enough jobs to keep us busy for now?" Po said slowly. It was an understatement. The trouble was, they had *too many* jobs. No wonder Gus looked like he was comin' down with somethin', all hot and bothered. They didn't even have enough time to be havin' this conversation, if Tilden had taken another job.

"That's not the point. Guess who that was that came in just now?" Tilden didn't give her time to answer. He tapped the clipboard with a finger, pointin' to a name. "Uriah Blackwood."

"Duchess Sheppard's brother?" she wondered, and

he nodded. "The crazy one that's always in the evenin' journals?"

"That's the one," Tilden said cheerfully. "And he just offered to pay us eleven hundred shields and some change to fix him a ship by Mead Moon mornin'."

Eleven hundred shields….that was three months' worth'a rent! Po squealed, grabbin' the clipboard to see the number in print for herself. There it was, signed for by a scratchy black signature and a stamp'a authentication. She bounced giddily on her toes. If they did this job, Po wouldn't have to quit school after all, at least not for a while! She could finish her Fourteenth year and then use the holiday to—

Her bouncin' slowed till she was flatfooted on the ground again, frownin' at the clipboard confusedly. She flipped the page over, then back.

"I don't get it. What's he need fixed?"

"Go on and tell her, then," Gus moaned, stoppin' with his hands dug into his hair. "Tell her what you told Blackwood we could fix even though every greedy Easterner mechanic turned him away with good reason."

Tilden took the clipboard from Po and took his time perusin' the form, avoidin' her eyes. "A Chimera class thermobird." He cleared his throat quietly. "With a Bylink 12-Twelve engine."

"A Chimera class—*Tilden*!" Po yelped, flappin' her hands at him as he cringed. He knew it was bad. Anyone who knew *anythin'* about engines would know it was bad, even if they didn't understand why. Tilden definitely did.

A Chimera was finicky enough. As pricey as a heliocraft on account'a bein' so deceptively pretty, and as fast as a Nyad—right up until it repaid you with stallin' at fifteen hundred feet. But a thermobird? A Chimera outfitted specifically for coastin' in the thermosphere, which meant it would fly like a bag'a cans everywhere else? Whose numptified idea had that been? She was flabbergasted. She couldn't even touch on the Bylink 12-Twelve. It was just plain unholy.

"Now, listen," Tilden said as she squawked wordlessly at him. "It's a payin' job. We don't have to approve'a what we're fixin', that's not our business. Even if..." He took a breath, enfoldin' the clipboard in his arms for stability. "...even if Chimeras are the ugliest junkers this side'a the Epimtheus and I swore on Ubber's grave I'd never set wrench to one."

Ubber was the family goat, who'd been dead some ten years. Po barely remembered him, but he'd become somethin' of a Trimble mascot. Whenever they needed somethin' to swear on, they used the flowery mound under the kitchen window and reminded each other that Ubber always came lookin' for promise breakers. Da had started the tradition. Po supposed that was kinda ironic, now.

"That ain't but half the problem," she said, sighin', and Gus bobbed his head in agreement. "A Bylink 12-Twelve...they don't even *make* most parts for those anymore! If he needs a—"

"He does," Gus interjected.

"And a...?" Po felt herself pale as he nodded again. "Does he at least have a workin'—"

"Nope."

"*Tilden!*"

"Eleven hundred shields, Po!" Tilden burst out, throwin' up his arms. She jumped back a step as Gus stopped walkin' and looked at Tilden in concern. "How could I say no to that, when it might mean..." Tilden trailed off, mouth workin', and dropped his hands, suddenly defeated.

Po's throat squeezed. She touched his arm to silently let him know he didn't need to go on. She understood; she wouldn't ask him to admit that he'd lied when he'd said they were fine. She didn't *want* to hear him admit it. Tilden was like Mum, who'd go on stubbornly pretendin' it wasn't rainin' right until the sky fell down. The moment either one'a them got out their umbrella, Po would know things weren't bad…they were worse.

Gus circled around the fan and joined them, uncertainly takin' the clipboard from Tilden. He chewed his lip for a minute, thin eyebrows pressed together. Po shot him a covert look as Tilden stared glumly at his scuffed boots, and he nodded just once, tightly.

"We might be able to hijack some galving links from a Pegasus," he suggested. His painful effort couldn't'a been any more obvious, but Tilden still perked up hopefully.

"That's what I thought," he said, walkin' quickly over to the wall'a spare parts, where he jumped up onto a stepladder and started rummagin' around, elbow-deep in the cubbyholes. "We get some new links and install a lower class fluctuator, it wouldn't even *be* a Bylink 12-Twelve anymore, and Blackwood wouldn't know the difference."

"Ain't that dishonest?" Po wondered.

"Replacin' his Bylink? We'd be doin' him a favor!" At Po's silence, Tilden glanced over his shoulder and sighed. "I'll tell him upfront, if it'd make you feel better. But he won't mind." She nodded, nonetheless grateful, and he dove back into the cubbies. Metal scraped and banged as he hunted through their stores.

"What are we gonna do about all our other jobs?" Gus asked, flinchin' at the ruckus Tilden was makin'.

"Finish 'em." A hand-sized spring rolled off a shelf and rattled to the floor. "Po, we'll need you to miss school tomorrow. You think you can swing it?"

"Yeah. Mum's not gonna like it though."

"She will when she hears about the money!" Tilden cackled.

Po wasn't so sure, but she left him to his illusions, too glad to see him happy and purposeful both at once. A little yellow sunlight seemed to be leakin' into the shop, poolin' out around Tilden, spreadin' his warmth. She wanted to edge closer to it, close her eyes and soak it in. She hadn't realized how drafty *Trimble and Sons* had become in recent months…hadn't realized she'd grown used to it, and let the cold become her normal.

With a vigorous clang, Tilden suddenly growled, "Bogrosh!"

"*Tilden!*" Po squeaked, aghast, although Gus actually snickered. It wasn't like Po didn't hear that kinda language all the time at The Owl, but Mum had a strict no-cursin' rule, and she somehow always knew when it had been broken.

Apparently, Tilden didn't care. "Bleedin'…will you look at this?" He spun down off'a the stepladder, tossin' somethin' at Gus, who fumbled to catch it with a grunt. "Gus, how many times have I told you not to fiddle with the fluctuators? You've shorted this one out."

Lookin' sheepish, Gus turned the brass metal cylinder over and over in his hands, and Po could tell he was just itchin' to do somethin' about the scraggly little wires corkscrewin' away from either end'a it. Tinkerin' with small, detailed parts that most people needed to get under a magnification glass to see clearly was soothin' for him. His hands did all the work, so his brain could just coast.

"We got others," Po reminded Tilden as he crossed his freckled arms and glared sourly at their backwards brother.

"That was the last C-class. We'll have to get another. Not to mention some half decent greasers and a transfusion conduit."

"We need more solder, too," Gus added, passin' the

fluctuator off to Po, like he didn't trust himself with it. She bounced the tube on her hand as Tilden jotted down a shoppin' list on a fresh piece'a parchment. He clucked his tongue, his eyes glazin' over as he entered the Trimble Trance.

"Benny's and the other dealers will already be closed for the night. I wonder if Mum would be willin' to shop for us tomorrow while we finish our work load?"

"Oh, Tilden, you can't ask her to do that on the day before festival!" Po chided. "She'll be wantin' to work on her biscuits to give out at North Pier!"

"She'd do it if we asked her," he said, frownin'.

"That's what I mean." Twice a year every year, on Mead Moon and Sterlin' Eve, Frances Trimble baked a good six dozen'a her famous chocolate biscuits to give the kids at North Pier orphanage. Po conjectured that Mum's heart was just too big for her body, and all the nice things she did for everyone else was how she coped with the excess. Still, she'd drop everythin' else she loved, all her good works, hospital visit and biscuits, in one beat'a her too-big heart if her kids asked her for anythin' that was in her power to give. It was a power Po thought it best to tap sparingly. "I'll go early to the dealers, I don't mind. We shouldn't trouble Mum when she's got…oh, what now?"

Gus and Tilden were grinnin' at each other, makin' her realize that siblin' alliances had shifted again. They often did.

"It's really too bad none'a us take after Mum, ain't it?" Gus said with a pointed look, foldin' his hands diplomatically in his lap. "Sure would get a lot more done if we had someone around who never thought about themselves."

Tilden laughed as Po stuck her tongue at him, and roped an arm around her neck, pullin' her into his warm, muscled side. "It's no wonder Bags and half the

Epimetheus argue about who's gonna marry you when you're not lookin'."

Po felt like she should be breathin' fire, her face was suddenly so hot. "They don't do that!"

"Well, maybe not yet," Tilden chuckled. He gave her shoulder a squeeze and gestured widely with his free hand, like he was paintin' an extravagant picture. "But you just wait. We fix this Chimera in time for Mead Moon, and mark me, Honora's gonna be singin' the Trimble family's praises!"

"And if we don't?" Gus asked, starin' doubtfully at Tilden's invisible paintin'.

Tilden grew sober. His hand loosened on Po's shoulder, like the thought'a that weakened him. And Po had to admit, as she looked around at the shop Da had built up from nothin' but a drawer full'a shields and his good reputation and thought about leavin' it, she felt a little wobbly too. As long as they had this shop, they had at least a part'a Da. The heart'a him. To Po, givin' it up meant acknowledgin' that he really wasn't comin' back…that he had nothin' to come back *for*.

A few months, he'd said. Then he would swoop in, pluck them off the farm and outta the slums, and they'd start a new life, a *good* life, somewhere else. Po hadn't wanted a new life. She'd been happy enough with the chickens and the tire heap in the backyard and the mornin's when it would be just the two'a them in the shop, tinkerin' away. But Da had made it sound easy and magical, and Gus and Tilden were old enough to take care'a *Trimble and Sons* while he was away, so they'd said goodbye and watched him fly away like he was sailin' off on some great adventure, to return with pirates' gold.

It had been two years, but Po couldn't concede defeat. Not on this. Gus and Tilden said that made her naïve; she said it made her hopeful. It didn't buy you much on the street or fill an empty stomach, but hope, it was the wheels'a the world, keepin' it turnin'. If no one was naïve and hopeful, she thought it would chug to a slow stop.

If no one ever hoped for anythin' to happen, then nothin' ever would.

It was near on midnight by the time the trolley deposited Po at the end'a the spindly gravel lane to the farmhouse. She was the very last passenger; Mitts and Wesley Grubhouse had gotten dropped off a mile back into the city, and they were the Trimbles' nearest neighbors. Po thumbed the copper cogs she'd borrowed from Tilden into the slotted till at the front'a the shuttle, and holdin' her bag over her head, stepped out into the rain that had come with dark. Sludge splashed up into her boots as she jogged down the drive, not wantin' to be alone in the dark, rainy countryside a minute longer than she had to. She loved the country, and she loved the rain, but hand-in-hand with the pitch black and the late hour, they were both unsettlin'. She kept her eyes on the flickerin' light on the wrap-around porch, her beacon. One'a the downstairs windows'a the leanin' white house glowed with firelight from the dyin' hearth, though she couldn't make out any smoke tricklin' from the stone chimney. She couldn't wait to hang her soaked socks from the mantel, curl up on her side, and finally sleep.

Poor Gus and Tilden. They'd decided to sleep on the rickety old cots in the back'a the shop so they could roll outta bed and right into their work boots. Mr. Blackwood was bringin' his Chimera in at six in the evenin', so that left them only 10 or so hours'a to wrap up their other jobs and prep for mechanical surgery on the Bylink. Po had offered to stay with them, but when Gus had sent Mum a log to fill her in on the situation (they'd drawn straws), she'd asked Po to come home instead. She was prolly gonna iron Po's ears about missin' school, but there'd be hugs, too, and biscuits, to curb the pain.

Po sped up, skippin' up the creaky porch steps as the oaks flankin' the drive rattled in the wind and the rain hissed angrily at her back. Fumblin' in her bag, she dug out her key, jammed it in the sky blue door, and hurried in outta the storm.

The black potbelly stove the Trimbles always warmed their shoes around wasn't lit, but Po stomped outta her boots and sat them at its clawed feet all the same. Her coat she flung over the banister'a the angular staircase standin' like a maypole at the heart'a the house. To its left was the wide open kitchen with its stout wooden table and jungle'a hangin' pots and pans. On its other side was the family room, and tucked under it like a pantry was the house's only head. It was the perfect setup for Gus and Tilden to chase Po in endless figure eights—startin' in the kitchen, passin' between the stairs and the stove, hurtlin' through the cozy family room, and loopin' around the stove and back in the other side'a the kitchen again and again. There were dents here and there where elbows, knees, and heads hadn't slowed enough before slidin' around a corner; with the exception'a the tiles in the entry way, the farmhouse had the same drafty wooden floors in every room. Runnin' around stockin'-footed was the surest way to test bone against hundred year old drywall.

Mum was dozin' on the sofa in front'a the fireplace, her pale hair spillin' off her pillow, white against blue. She cracked her eyes as Po backed up to the fireplace with a shiver and a sigh.

"You're late," she murmured, closin' her eyes again. They were brown like Gus's and Po's, only with thick eyelashes the same dark color as her eyebrows. Po envied her those eyelashes, and her lips, which were small and curvy where Po's were large and uniform. "I made tea.

It's likely cold by now."

"That's alright." Po shuffled, givin' her front a turn with the fire as she wrung out her hair. A sundry assortment'a frames fought for space on the mantelpiece, their black and white kinetic stills overlappin' each other. She picked out her favorite and sat it front and center where it belonged. Somehow, it always ended up migratin' to the back, behind the still'a little Gus holdin' a huge, glassy-eyed trout. In the still, she was four years old, bucktoothed and beamin'. Mum and Da held her between them, laughin' and lookin' happy, young, and beautiful. Mum was still beautiful, but her face didn't light up like that anymore. Nowadays, her features seemed lost in a shadow.

"You three get caught up on your work?" Mum yawned.

Po wedged her thumbnail into the edge'a the frame, pickin' at dust. "Mostly. We've still got a big haul for tomorrow, but I think we can swing it."

"Never thought I'd see a Chimera in that old shop. Your father'd be wheezin' into a paper bag if he was here, bless him."

Po's thumb stilled; she pulled back her hand, turnin' curiously. Mum must be half asleep, if she was talkin' like that about Da.

Mum was still a minute. Then, as if feelin' Po's stare, she raised a beckonin' hand. Po peeled off her socks, hung them from one'a the nailheads dottin' the mantel, and tiptoed over to join her, layin' down with her face to the fire and her back to Mum's distant expression.

Wrappin' a loose arm around her, Mum asked, "How's school?"

"It's alright."

"Your marks alright?"

Po hesitated. "Most'a them."

"Piano?"

"Tutor Clevenger said it sounds like someone's bludgeonin' the keys with a kitchen sink when I play."

Mum's laugh unrolled into sleepy silence. After a time, she murmured, "You just keep doin' your best, even if it makes the ivories bleed."

"Alright." Po watched the fire curl and twirl fitfully. A little seed'a what she wanted to say throbbed inside'a her, like somethin' lodged in her throat. The longer she avoided sayin' it, the more she felt she had to, and the more she dreaded makin' herself. "Momma," she ventured finally. Mum hummed. "I know what you're gonna say, but I've been thinkin' about this a lot, and I think it makes good sense. Say I don't quit The Owl. Say…I only take a year off, to help us get our feet under us after this Chimera business. I could help Gus and Tilden until they can afford to bring in an outsider."

Mum's deep breathin' grew quiet and thoughtful. "What do you think I'm gonna say?"

"No," Po admitted, cringin'.

"And why?"

"Because I've got a chance for a real education, and you want me to take it, to give myself more options."

"Do you think that's untrue or unfair?"

"Well, no. But I don't think I need more options, either. I wanna be an airship mechanic, and I can do that right in the shop."

"Forever?" Mum wondered flatly.

"I guess so."

There was a note'a heartbreak in Mum's whisper as she stroked Po's arm. "It's best not to guess about forever, Po."

Po frowned at the fire, her eyes feelin' heavy and dry. Forever was one'a those slippery words that could be good or bad dependin' on how you said it, but right now, to her sleepy mind, it mostly sounded big and far away, like somethin' she shouldn't have to worry about for a long time yet. She nestled her face into the scratchy wool couch.

"I'm just sayin'…can we talk about it, sometime?"

"Aren't we talkin' about it now?"

"Momma."

"Well, you already guessed my feelin's," Mum pointed out. "And no amount'a talkin' is gonna change those." After a stubborn moment, she sighed, ticklin' the wispy hairs on the back'a Po's neck. "But I know they don't always make sense. You workin' at the shop—if it's what you want—does. I'm not sayin' yes yet. I don't want you rushin' into somethin' you could regret in a few years' time, when all the other Eighteens are graduatin'. But ask me again tomorrow."

Seein' as she'd been thinkin' things over for a year now, Po didn't think this could possibly count as *rushin'*, but she nodded as she yawned. Usually Mum literally stomped a foot when she tried bringin' this up. The sluggish fire and sad patter'a rain must'a put her in a thoughtful mood, and Po didn't want to shatter it by bein' quarrelsome. It was enough that Mum was at least willin' to consider what she'd said. Besides…it was hard to be quarrelsome with one foot in her dreams and the other not a step behind.

She drifted off to sleep, feelin' hopeful.

III

The rain kept up through the night and into
mornin'. It fell in slow, fat drops, like it was too tired to
make itself stop. Outside'a Po's tiny bedroom window, it
plinked into the empty tin buckets she would end up usin'
to carry scratch out to the chicken coops. It was a lonely
sort'a sound, but she liked wakin' up to it.

She could hear Mum already hard at work in the
kitchen, probably gettin' a head start on her biscuits. Pots
and pans clanged; a wooden spoon rapped a counter
determinedly. The public locomotive rumbled the
farmhouse as it cut through the field behind the tire mounds
like it did every mornin' at this time. Po stared up at her
ceilin', unbothered by the way her narrow bed ticked back
and forth on its legs, squeakin'. For a second, she listened
to the dissonant chorus and smiled. She'd missed this. The
Owl was always so quiet before eight in the mornin',
almost hushed. On the Trimble farm, a person was lucky to
sleep a wink past six.

She wrapped her quilt around her shoulders like a
shawl, then wobbled after the sounds'a Mum wreckin'
havoc on her biscuits. The wooden stairs were cold, makin'
her toes curl as she waded into the grey mornin' light
floodin' the mudroom and the kitchen.

At the table, Mum had lined up all her mixin'
bowls and was purposefully dividin' ingredients between
them. She'd tied her silvery hair back in a loose braid that
swung like a pendulum over her shoulder as she reached
from bowl to bowl with cups'a flour and sugar. Aside from
her dusted green apron, she didn't look like much of a
cook—she was still wearin' the work boots she'd probably

worn out to milk Dregs at first daylight, along with her brown coveralls and quilted purple coat—but Po knew better.

"Mornin'," Mum greeted distractedly as she moved down the row'a bowls with teaspoons'a salt. Po pulled out a chair and sat, huggin' her knees to her chest. "Gus said you're goin' to the market for them today. You need me to come with you?"

Po shook her head. She inched a finger towards the lip of a bowl with a little overflow, but Mum swatted her down.

"I need six eggs. Find me eight, and I'll make you some breakfast."

"I don't think there are gonna be that many," Po said, doubtful as she glanced out at the rain.

"There are nine," Mum predicted without lookin' away from her work, wavin' for Po to do as she was told.

There was a pair'a clunky boots by the back door. Groanin', Po limped over and pulled them on, then slipped Da's long leather duster off its peg and buttoned it up over her nightgown. She thumped out into the rain, less enthusiastic about it now. The buckets under her bedroom window were nearly full before she tipped them over and carried them to the straw sack'a feed in the dilapidated wagon bed by Mum's vegetable garden. After shovelin' out some grain, she made for the long, low coop at the back'a the yard where the grass was tall and weedy, right next to the tire heap. The pyramid'a old wheels had been there for as long as Po could remember, but she'd never climbed it. Too many'a the wheels were rusty and torn.

She had to duck her head to get into the coop. The rain on the slanted metal roof sounded like tinny applause. Fat little hens scrambled outta her way while others clucked warmly at her from their roosts against the wall.

"I'm here for your eggs," Po informed them as she

scattered the feed. "Me and the orphans are gonna eat them all."

But they seemed more interested in their food than her dark prophecy. As they pecked the floor clean, she peeked through their roosts, patting the straw gently. In a few short minutes, she'd collected not nine, but *ten* small brown eggs in the deep pockets'a Da's coat.

Mum smiled knowingly and eyed the bulgin' pockets as Po stomped in outta the rain, leavin' her boots on the back step. She held out a bowl for the eggs, then instructed, "Wash your hands when you're done."

Breakfast was an oozin' cheese and egg pie, chased down with a glass'a fresh blueberry juice. Mum served it without losing her mesmerizin' rhythm, dancin' between her dishes, sendin' up a cloud'a flour in her wake.

"What dealers are you seein' this mornin'?"

"Benny's, Milf's, and Sam's, at least," Po said thickly, swallowin'. She stared thoughtfully at the wooden crossbeams on the ceilin'. It had been a while since she'd had to make a market run, and she'd never made one on her own. But she knew enough about bargainin', talkin' sweet and playin' hard-to-get in turns, to not be nervous. "Benny's will have the best fluctuators, but his greasers are the priciest in the city. I'm hopin' Sam will have a transfusion conduit in the right class. If he doesn't…I might have to go eastward."

Mum gave one'a her lumps'a dough a solid slap. "Let's hope not. They'll charge you to the heavens. Maybe I should come with you after all."

"That's alright," Po quickly assured her. If Mum came with her, there'd be no question'a who would do the bargainin' and bullyin', and Po needed the practice. "I know you gotta a lot'a bakin' to do. I can manage."

Mum nodded, though she didn't look precisely pleased. She got a cup down from one'a the overhead cupboards and started usin' it to punch circles in the chocolate-colored dough, which she then flipped over onto a tarnished baking pan. "I hope you're not missin' anythin' important at school today."

"Tutor Agnes said I could skip if I needed to." When Mum only frowned, Po added, "She said Headmaster Eldritch would like to meet me sometime. He's impressed with my work."

"'Course he is," Mum said, settin' down the cup and turnin' with a smile to look at her. "I told him he would be, if he let you in. When your father and I went to interview with him about enrollin' you, he put up such a fight, you'd think…" She shook her head, at a loss. "I'll never understand Easterners like him."

"They're not all bad. Even the bad ones…I just don't think they understand what it's like, westward."

"That's true, they don't," Mum agreed sadly, pushin' her bangs outta her forehead with the back'a her wrist and leavin' a streak'a flour behind. "And we can't blame them for that, can we? Help me get these biscuits in the oven. Take a pan. And mind you don't get grabby with the dough."

After breakfast, Po washed down in the water closet and pulled on one'a her drab olive jumpsuits and her yellow raincoat, glad to be outta The Owl's stiflin' uniform. As she brushed the snarls from her hair, she called up Tilden and Gus at the shop, usin' the log interface in the family room. The shoebox-sized device hung on the wall between two cuckoo clocks, which made makin' calls on the hour a bit of a feat. She turned the wire speaker mouth towards her as the square black and white screen flickered awake.

She dropped her hairbrush. A scene'a utter chaos greeted her. Gus, lookin' into the lens with wild eyes and oil-stained hands, stood against a background'a smoke.

Parts were heaped in precarious piles on either side'a him, metal limbs pointin' at the sky. Po could hear Tilden shoutin' and bangin' away at somethin'. It looked like an airship slaughterhouse.

"What happened?" Po gasped into her hands.

"We fired up one'a the Nyads that were brought in this mornin'. No one told us it had a bad turbine."

"*No*. Did it—"

"Yeah."

"Did you—"

"We tried."

"How about—"

"Po," Gus said curtly, and flinched as Tilden shouted again. "I gotta get back to work. Why are you still home?"

Po bit her lip and folded her hands over her stomach, which felt upset of a sudden. "Just wanted to make sure there wasn't anythin' else we needed what wasn't on Tilden's list."

He laughed a little manically and reached to cut his end'a the connection. "Twelve more hours."

Po skipped out on brushin' the rest'a her hair, packin' up her things instead. She shouldn't'a taken her time with the chickens and breakfast—clearly Gus and Tilden had been up at least as long as Mum, if they'd even slept at all. She shoved her allowance from Tilden along with his list and the trolley pass she'd purchased last night into her satchel and tossed it over her shoulder, hurtlin' at the door with her bootlaces halfway undone. Mum beat her there, blockin' her way with a paper bag and a forbiddin' look.

"Let me pull your hair back for you before you go."

"Momma—"

"You can't look like a school girl if you're gonna be barterin' with the big boys. It'll take half a moment."

Mum forced the paper bag into her hands. It was warm and lumpy, and smelled'a glorious chocolate biscuits hot outta the oven. "Turn around."

With a longsufferin' sigh, Po turned. As Mum's fingers combed swiftly but softly through her tangles, she asked, "Make it like yours?"

"I'll make it prettier than mine."

"I like yours. Please?"

With a tug and a twist, Mum relented.

"You're *out*? You don't even have *one* C-class fluctuator? I'd take a broken one!"

Benny gave Po an impatient look as he double-checked his handheld datascope, tappin' its screen with a writin' wand. The silver datascope looked tiny in his monstrous hands, like a toy paddle, but he handled the wand almost delicately.

"Nope," he said after a minute, shruggin', his shoulders stretchin' his button-up work shirt. In her stupefied daze, Po noted that his blond braid was almost as long as hers, if skinnier. She wondered why he kept it when it made his square chin seem even bigger. "Sold my last one this mornin'. You can tell Tilden he picked a bad day to stock up."

"He's not stockin' up," Po said, pleadin'. "We need that part for a custom fix!" She squeezed against the brick wall as two'a Benny's hired hands pressed by, carryin' a smolderin' heat conduit in their gloved hands. If the Trimble's shop was half as busy as Benny's, Po hoped Gus and Tilden thought to close her—otherwise, they'd never get caught up.

Benny's was smaller than the Trimbles', because he didn't fix ships—just supplied the people who did with parts and the like. Instead'a havin' a barn for workspace, he had a low-ceilinged brick warehouse for engine trappin's. Po could have wandered the labrynth'a shelves and run her fingers over springs and greasers for hours, admirin' all the pretties Benny overcharged for. She couldn't believe in all that there wasn't *one* C-class fluctuator left in the place. It wasn't even that rare a part!

Settin' down his datascope, Benny planted his hands and leaned heavily against the counter, loomin' over Po. Not in a threatenin' way…just in a way that was inevitable, on account him bein' so huge. She used to ride into this shop on Da's shoulders; most'a the fellows here had known her since her toddlin' years.

"What's he need a C-class for?" Benny asked.

Po grimaced. "A Chimera."

He gave a visible shudder. "What possessed him?"

"It's good money," Po said, defensive, and Benny grunted.

"Hard to argue with that." Holdin' out a hand for the list Po had crinkled in dismay, he said, "Let's see that list." He scanned it briefly, then cursed, reached into his chest pocket, and pulled out a pair'a half-moon spectacles that sat on the very tip'a his nose. He frowned. "You're plannin' on gettin' your greasers from Milf?"

Po had intentionally written that down, hopin' either Benny or Sam would see it. She feigned embarrassment as she tugged the list outta his hand and folded it up. "Well, it's all we can really afford right now. Ain't nothin' personal, Benny. Tilden and Gus just said that Milf's would be a little more worth the shields, in the end."

Benny pulled off his bifocals and folded them very slowly, his frown deepenin'. "They said that?"

"Well, *somethin'* like that. I'm sure they'd buy from you if they could. Especially since Milf's has been doin' so well lately…did you hear about him gettin' that special order from Duke Sheppard himself?"

"I heard," Benny said flatly. Po noticed his grip wasn't quite so gentle when he picked up his datascope this time. "Now, listen here, Little Trimble, what if I made it worth your while? You need what, three greasers? You buy five, and I'll cut you a deal, special. One hundred and eighty shields for the lot."

Po brightened, opened her mouth, and cringed. "That sounds like an awfully good deal. Only I don't think we're gonna be needin' five, and we can't pay just to have 'em sittin' in storage, you know?"

Eyein' her, Benny folded his arms. "You can never have enough greasers."

"Well…" Fumblin' a bit, Po opened her satchel and flipped through her money. This was the tricky part. The key to bargainin' wasn't to make giant leaps in your offers, but to win an extra ten shields here and five shields there, enough to maybe buy a whole extra part at the end'a the day. "Maybe I could do the five greasers for one twenty…I think Tilden would say that was alright."

"I can't do one twenty, but I'd part with 'em for one fifty."

Bitin' her lip, Po put the money away regretfully. "I'm sorry, Benny, but Milf's gonna give us just the three we need for one hundred flat. I think I'd better do that. I've got a lot still to get today."

Benny's eyes were on the stack'a shields she was takin' her time tuckin' into her bag. She'd nearly finished buttonin' it when he suddenly barked, "One thirty, then."

"Done!" Po squealed, giddy. She hopped once and clapped her hands together under her chin. "How did I do?"

Benny shook his head, but smiled in a tight line. "Fair. Though I wouldn't take out so much at once—don't want to tempt the sticky fingers, eh?" He reached under the counter and slid a form over to her as she counted out his money. "Want those pushed straight to the shop?"

"Yes, please."

"It'll take a while. We've been havin' trouble makin' deliveries with the traffic as it is."

Po wrinkled her nose, but nodded as she carefully signed the form. There was no worse day to go shoppin' in Caldonia than the day before Mead Moon, when everyone had last minute errands to be about before the holiday shut half the planet down. It had taken her trolley an hour alone just to push into the teemin' wall'a busyness. She wasn't lookin' forward to settin' out for Sam's, but if anyone had a C-class fluctuator, he would.

He didn't. Neither did Milf, Jaren, or Hundley.

By early afternoon, Po was startin' to feel sick with worry. She sat down on an iron bench in front'a fan emporium with her packed lunch and picked at it, tossin' scraps to the owls watchin' her from the corner'a their eyes. Before long, she had a whole flock'a little albino screechers sharin' her bench and makin' her look like a genuine bird lady.

She'd managed to get the greasers, solder, and a half-decent transfusion conduit sent to the shop, but none'a Tilden's usual Westerner suppliers had the fluctuator, and the Chimera couldn't so much as yawn without one. Po'd even thought to ask after a B-class, thinkin' she could make one work with the right mods, but it seemed Caldonia was just plum outta fluctuators.

It made sense. Mead Moon's crownin' climax was at sundown. Honora's three full moons came out early— usually in late afternoon—but as the sun melted into the horizon, Telesto, Nyx, and Atlas began to truly glow, green, red, and pearlescent white. At about that time, every ship citywide would launch to enjoy the view from the thermosphere. It was supposed to be spectacular.

Fluctuators allowed ships to hover in the thermosphere without their engines floodin'. If there weren't any left on Western main, it was because everyone was makin' sure their airship was up to the challenge'a hoverin' for hours on end. They should've thought'a this!

Po chewed her biscuit woodenly and swallowed it down with the lump in her throat. In five hours, she'd combed Western Main from the smokestacks on the river to the lumber factory at the edge'a town. There was nothin' for it; she was gonna have to search *real* main street…Eastern Main. Which wouldn't be so bad if she didn't know for a fact she would stick out there like a heliocraft in a room full'a aethercopters. She was fairly used to stickin' out at The Owl, where there were so few Westerners, but it was the mean people she just couldn't abide. And Eastern Main would have plenty'a those.

If she just had one other person to take with her, it wouldn't be half so bad.

She followed that thought all the way back to Bags's corner'a Western Main. She stayed close behind him as he wheeled his cart with its folded-up umbrella into the alleyway by his Mum's bakery, where he locked its wheels to hooks in the brick road. Pullin' his cap out from behind his back and settlin' it nobly on his head, he turned to face her, lookin' pleased with himself.

"Now then," he said, and offered her his elbow, "where to?"

She hooked her arm through his and took a step in the right direction. "There's a shop right where Rose Avenue crosses main. Shouldn't be more than six or seven blocks away."

"Well, that ain't naught but a stroll in the park." Wigglin' his hand in his coat pocket for a minute, Bags pulled out a wrapped pastry and proffered it to her as if she'd asked for it.

"I already ate," Po objected, but still reached for the pastry, findin' herself suddenly famished. A fresh burst'a optimism could do that to a person. Now that she was excited and sure she'd find what she needed on Eastern Main, it was much easier to enjoy the moist, crumbly crust'a the pastry and its warm jelly fillin'. She licked her fingers clean with a smile.

The festival was celebrated city-wide, but it became obvious as Po and Bags drew close to Main Street that the Easterners had celebratin' down to a fine if chaotic art. Horse-drawn carriages, bimotors and automobiles packed Eastern Caldonia's deep and narrow alleyways, while the city's roads were reserved for sidewalk sales and automata displays, for corner stages promisin' acrobats, musicians, fire eaters, magicians. Tomorrow at this time, every type a vendor sellin' every type'a food would be pushin' their carts through the crowds or else holdin' up their wares on weathervane-like contraptions, danglin' candied apples and tufts'a cotton candy. The air would be a soup of a thousand different smells, organic and mechanic, like the streets would be a stew of a thousand different types'a people, Easterners, Westerners, chocolate-skinned Zenovians, blue-eyed Pantedans, and even a few Freherians—or Frers, as they liked to be called—dressed in black like Vees.

The first shop Po and Bags tried was fresh outta fluctuators, but Po figured they might be, bein' so close to Rose Avenue still. She and Bags got a short list'a other sellers and some brief directions and headed back out into the pre-holiday hubbub without feelin' too uneasy yet.

"So was your fancy school cancelled for the holiday?" Bags asked as they waited at a crosswalk for a trolley to rumble by.

"No. But I got permission to miss."

"I thought they was made'a stricter stuff than that."

Po looked at him, holdin' her hair behind her ear as the trolley stirred up a warm breeze. She never could tell if her Westerner friends hated The Owl or secretly dreamed of it, but Bags seemed to be genuinely confused as he stared skyward as if tryin' to make out the school on its white moon.

"Tell me about it," he insisted, leadin' her across the trolley tracks. "What sort'a stuff do you learn? How many spoons to eat with, that sorta thing?"

"Bags," Po laughed as she skipped from one track to the other, "why would my da have sent me there to learn about airships if I was just gonna learn about *spoons*?"

"Maybe he didn't know. No offense to your da, o'course. They could'a pulled a fast one on him."

"Not on *my* da. He knew. He liked The Owl. He worked with them a lot, helped them keep their bus-ships in good order. He would never have sent me if he didn't think they could show me somethin' about ships he couldn't."

"And did they?"

Somethin' bit at Po's heart as she realized the answer. They had. Which meant she'd already surpassed what Da would've been able to teach her on his own, which meant if she left The Owl now, she was still better off than if she'd never gone. She was already handier with ships than Gus and Tilden, though neither'a them would likely admit it short'a bein' held at gunpoint.

Was that her decision, then? It felt like she'd been siftin' for excuses all day. But excuses to leave The Owl? Or excuses to stay?

Three stores later, the pastry Po had eaten was turnin' somethin' awful in her stomach. Bags tried to calm her down as she whimpered and paced outside their latest stop, an especially fancy establishment with white tile floors and walls. What kind'a numpty put down white tiles in a parts shop but didn't even carry fluctuators? The woman behind the counter had laughed in their faces and shooed them out with a lace fan.

"Now, Po," Bags said in a soothin' voice. He kept tryin' to lay his hands on her shoulders, but she was turnin' circles too fast.

"What am I gonna do?" she gasped, clutchin' her braid. "Gus and Tilden are gonna dip me in oil! The Chimera's gonna be there any time now. They need that fluctuator before they can do anythin' else to it! Oh, we're jammed!"

Bags finally caught her by the arm and carefully led her to a bench, where he sat her down. He kept his hand on her forearm, like he didn't trust her not to spring right back to her feet, and chewed his lip thoughtfully. "Why don't you just make one?"

"Make one? From scratch?" Po squeaked. Her trapped arm spasmed as she tried to throw it up in desperation. "I could, maybe. But not in less than seven or eight hours. I don't know anyone who could, except maybe…" Inspiration rang in Po's head like a deafenin' bell toll. She gasped again. "I need to send a log!"

Lookin' around, Bags stood and pointed to a corner street box, built more like a booth, with a log interface against its back wall. A few cogs and failed attempts to work the fancy interface later, Po waited for The Owl's operator to redirect her log to the campus workshop. After a few forbodin' beeps, the small square screen over Po's lens lit up with Tutor Agnes's flat expression.

"Ms. Trimble," Agnes greeted, her keen eyes narrowin' at Bags, who stood at Po's shoulder. Bags wisely yanked off his hat and stood at attention. "I thought you were assisting your brothers with their shop today."

"I am." Po quickly explained her dilemma and tried

not to wilt in shame when Agnes actually had to fan herself at the mention'a the Chimera.

"Fool boys," the old woman muttered. "If I've said it once, I've said it a hundred times. The only thing Bylinks are good for is—"

"Lookin' pretty before they kill you," Po finished from memory. "I know. I told them. But Tilden thinks with a new transfusion conduit—"

Agnes snorted loud enough to cut her off. It sounded like static comin' through the speaker box. "You can put a pig in a pie, but that doesn't make it an apple."

Picturing a pig pie with her stomach frazzled as it was wasn't exactly advantageous. Po glanced at Bags for help, but he was practicin' sinkin' into the sidewalk, where Agnes couldn't glare at him.

"Do you think you can do it?" she asked Agnes nervously. "Do you think you could build us a C-class fluctuator in time? We'd pay you for your troubles. And I could stay after school and help you in the workshop. And I could show the headmaster anything you liked!"

Sighin', Agnes folded her arms at the bottom edge'a the screen and gave Po a look that had been known to make ships magically fix themselves. "As it happens," she said finally, "I know a Pantedan collector who has a weakness for fluctuators. I'll get you your C-class and bring it to you at the shop."

Slappin' her hands over her mouth, Po laughed, silly with relief. "I can come get it!" she offered.

"No. It will be faster if you don't have to make a roundtrip journey to Atlas. Besides. I daresay I know a thing or two about Chimeras that Tilden should hear for the next time he decides to pluck your family out of the frying pan and plop you artlessly into the fire."

IV

The little red bell on the shop door dinged, and Po, Gus and Tilden swapped a nervous three-way look before filin' into the waitin' area from the shop proper to greet their distinguished guest. Po checked her braid and dusted her jumpsuit while Tilden clutched his clipboard and Gus fiddled mindlessly with a wad'a tangled springs. This was it. The clock was tickin'; the Chimera was here.

Her owner was a certifiable giant. Po had seen a lot'a big Pantedans, but the duchess's brother, Uriah Blackwood, wasn't big after the Pantedan fashion. He was just *tall*. He stood before the counter with his fingers lightly curled about its edge. His nails were long, manicured, and bejeweled every one'a them. She craned her neck to find his face. It was a peculiar face, pointed and mustached. His head looked too small for his body, but that might'a been an illusion created by his puffy fur coat, which was as black as his name and probably long enough to blanket Po's whole bed.

"Welcome back, Mr. Blackwood," Tilden said, takin' care to smooth out his Westerner drawl a bit. "Are you ready for us to take your ship?"

Mr. Blackwood laughed—a sound that almost seemed to bubble up outta him unbidden as he glanced around idly. "Oh yes, quite ready. Quite! What's that? Speak up, if you please, I had a rifle go off rather near my head this morning and I'm afraid I still have a buzz. What's that? What did you say?"

"Er, I said 'good'," Tilden answered, the back'a his ears goin' pink. He hadn't said anythin' at all.

Po frowned. For all she'd spent the last ten hours

frettin' about gettin' back to *Trimble and Sons* with the fluctuator on time, Mr. Blackwood was a whole three hours late. Which worked out fine—he had given Tutor Agnes time to drop off the C-class fluctuator and give Tilden an earful besides—but to think…all that worryin'…

Blackwood turned his back to them and spread his arms wide. "My coat, if you please."

Blinkin' at each other, Gus and Tilden hurried around the counter and workin' together, peeled the coat down the length'a his stringy arms.

"Careful now, don't let it drag. That's shobrek fur. Imported, you know."

Behind Blackwood's back, Gus and Tilden flailed at each other as Tilden ordered Gus to do somethin' with the coat that was probably worth more than the farmhouse and Gus refused, showin' him the oil on his hands. Sighin' at them, Po held out her hands for the coat. It didn't feel like shobrek. It felt like run'a the mill marten fur.

"Are you havin' your ship brought in by hovernet?" Gus asked as Blackwood turned, dustin' off his waistcoat. "'Cause we can scroll back the ceilin' and bring some lights up for your men."

"Hovernet, yes, I'll have them lower it in. Where will I be taking my dinner while I wait? I'm starved. Famished!" Blackwood exclaimed, wrigglin' his fingers at them. Gus's mouth wagged soundlessly.

"Your ship won't actually be done till tomorrow, Mr. Blackwood," Po said gently as Blackwood glanced at her, seemin' confused. It occurred to her that the things the evenin' journals all said about Uriah Blackwood bein' off his hat might actually be true. A big man with a little brain, they said. She felt suddenly sorry for him as she offered him back his coat. "But we'll have her in sparklin' order well in time for the Festival, just you wait."

"Alright," Blackwood conceded, disappointed. He

accepted his coat and gave another one'a his out of place laughs. "Say, make her actually sparkle, and I'll throw in a few extra cogs so you can fix your doorbell, hmm?"

"What's wrong with the doorbell?"

He absently bowed goodbye. "What's that? Oh. The doorbell. It doesn't ring." He let himself out with a ding, and Gus instantly buried his face in his hands, snortin'. Po poked him.

"Don't be mean," she scolded. "He—" She paused, listenin' with a tipped head to a distant thrum. "They're bringin' her in!"

The three'a them hurried back into the shop, throwin' up the barn lights and turnin' on the automated retractors for the paneled ceilin' on their way. As the ceilin' loudly ground back on its wheels, two small Nyads with a mesh metallic net pulled taut between them lowered their prize into the room. Tilden hurried to get on the com and direct the pilots towards the open space he and Gus had made in the middle'a the barn.

When the Chimera had been deposited and the Nyads neatly zipped back out into the dusky sky, Po stood with her brothers flankin' her and stared long and hard at the package. Tilden crouched down to study her from a different angle while Gus disappeared back into the waitin' room—possibly to find a paper baggie to breathe into.

The Chimera—branded *Lady Isabelle* just under her port wing—was pretty enough; sleek and clean, at least on the outside. Eggshell white and flat and wide, she looked almost like someone had dropped an anvil on her. Unfortunately, no one had. The bird was glitchy all on her own.

"See," Tilden said hoarsely as he stood and dusted his hands, "she don't look so bad."

Gus's groan carried in from the other room.

Po cautiously approached the ship, trailin' a light

hand across one'a the moon-shaped wings. She stooped beside the hull, felt around where the wing met the fuselage, and pulled the lever her fingers eventually found. A panel hissed open above her head, an exterior access point to the Bylink 12-Twelve. She *tsked*.

"Look at you," she murmured to the jumble'a parts that looked like they'd been thrown pell-mell into a pile'a glue. "I've seen bowls'a noodles less tangled than this mess. How do you even breathe?"

Tilden's shadow rippled over Po as he circled the ship. "What do you think?" he asked quietly, probably to keep Gus from overhearin' the note'a doubt in his voice.

Po bit her lip, stood, and unsheathed the wrench on her tool belt. "I think we'd better get started."

Sunlight marched over the cement floor like the frontlines of an army. Po watched it creep closer and closer, every inch a minute lost. Exhaustion pulled at her eyelids even though she was on her third cup'a tea since midnight. But then, goin' by the orange light kissin' the handle'a her tin mug, midnight was a long time gone.

It was officially the day'a the Mead Moon Festival, and *Lady Isabelle* was still puttin' off fumes and an oily burnt smell when Tilden pedaled her levelers. They had less than a quarter of a clock face to figure out why she was rejectin' her new fluctuator, and less clues than Po had empty cups'a tea. But that was the nice thing about all'a them bein' so tired. They'd stopped panickin', and now were just determined to see the thing done so they could go home and sleep.

Tilden's tousled blond head rose over the fuselage as he suddenly stood in *Isabelle's* cockpit. Her canopy window split down the middle and opened on hinges like a clam…one'a the Chimera's sillier features. And Po had compiled quite a list, these last ten hours.

"Anythin'?" he called, despondent, glowerin' at the muffin in his hand. Bags had stopped by an hour ago with a basket full'a sweets, but the way Gus and Tilden had looked at them, you'd think the muffins were laced with low grade turbine oil. Po hoped poor Bags didn't take bein' called a shifty-eyed ginghoo personally. At this rate, *Lady Isabelle* was likely to get a suitor before Po ever did.

Po pouted at the same square'a hardware she'd been starin' at all night, sittin' cross-legged under *Isabelle's* wing. The colors'a the wires were startin' to run together in her bleary vision, but she didn't need her sight to smell the forbodin' stink comin' off her half'a the engine. It would be even worse where Gus was neck-deep in the starboard parts.

"More'a the same," she replied. "It don't make sense. Maybe we could try reroutin' the heat generator? I don't know what else could make a smell like that."

"I checked its serial. It was bought new with the ship not a year ago."

"Shoddy Easterner mechanics," Gus chipped in from somewhere on the other side'a the ship, and coughed.

Po slumped, elbows on her knees, fists pushin' into her cheeks. "Ubber's gonna come for you, Tilden Harvey Trimble. You should never have promised Mr. Blackwood we could do this." Either Tilden didn't hear her, or he was choosin' to ignore her. He sat down in the cockpit without comment.

The doorbell suddenly chimed. For a moment, Po and her brothers were completely still and silent; Po could hear the cracklin' buzz'a photon power in the distant overhead lights. Frownin', she slowly stood.

"Gus," she asked in a hushed voice, "didn't you lock up last night after Blackwood left?"

He came around the side'a the ship, lookin'

disheveled and sheepish and with his hair all a mess, about twelve years old. "I guess I forgot."

Po shivered. The thought'a the front door bein' open to the rough-and-tumble Rose Avenue and its after-hour lurkers was unsettlin'. The cash till was up there. And she doubted they would'a heard the bell at all if they'd been hammerin' or runnin' a thermal torch.

Tilden bravely hopped outta the cockpit and after shootin' Gus a look'a lofty disgust, went to find out who was callin' so early in the mornin'. Maybe it was just Mum come to check on them.

Tryin' to shake off her jitters—which weren't helped by the amount'a tea bubblin' in her veins—Po knelt by *Isabelle's* wing, tired and daunted. She raised her trusty wrench by rote and then dropped it like an all-thumbs Eleven when Tilden's voice declared, "Mr. Blackwood! You're early!"

"Well, yes, but I noticed the open sign in the window, you see. I thought, you know, they wouldn't be open for business unless they were ready for the Mead Moon Festival. And that's today! This morning, in point of fact!"

There was a pause. Po imagined Tilden slowly leaning to one side to see around Mr. Blackwood's and determine whether or not Gus really had left the open sign up all night. He cleared his throat tellingly. Gus materialized by Po's elbow, horrified. She dazedly watched his fingers methodically twig and tweak the stragglin' wires'a the dead contraptor she'd fished outta the Chimera's rear joint coils.

"That was actually a mistake, Mr. Blackwood," Tilden said. "But we *are* nearly done with *Lady Isabelle*. I'd say in another hour or two, we—"

"And hour or two?" Blackwood repeated, sounding confused. "But I'm here *now*. Don't you promise to deliver on time, *every* time? At the cost of…your cost?"

"Y…yes, but if you look right here on the form you signed—"

"Oh yes, I see. Eleven hundred shields. That's what I agreed to pay, isn't it? Was it not enough? I suppose I could do thirteen hundred. But only if the ship was done. Did you say it was done?"

Po covered her face with her hands. If ever there was a time when bein' able to send logs from brain to brain would'a come in handy, this was it. She tried willin' Tilden to hear her and Gus holdin' their breath and throwin' silently-screamed no's his way. The wires under Gus's fiddlin' fingers went *tick tick* as he plucked at them. Ironically, the sound reminded Po'a coins plunkin' into a till.

In a shrill voice, Tilden said, "Yes, yes it is! It'll take just a few moments to…to go over all the mods with you so you can sign off on 'em…"

Takin' a deep breath, Po gripped Gus's wrist and mouthed, "Go help Tilden stall!"

"What are you gonna do?" he whispered as in the waitin' room, Tilden launched into a detailed description'a every step they'd taken with the Chimera in the last ten hours and then some.

Po closed the secondary panel and determinedly stood, starin' at the open maw'a the cockpit like it was a creature ready to swallow her whole. "I'm gonna make her listen to me."

Head bobbin' wildly, Gus dropped the contraptor at his feet and bolted.

It was just Po and *Isabelle* now, alone in the barn with nothin' but a wrench to separate them. Po's heartbeat was as even as her footsteps as she climbed the stepladder to the cockpit. She was in the Trimble Trance. Her mind was calm, just…busy. Thinkin'a what she could possibly do to make the Chimera behave, thinkin'a what would happen if she failed and Blackwood didn't pay them, thinkin'a someone else ownin' the shop, and Da comin' back but not recognizin' the place. Her jaw ached. She wanted to cry, but she knew once she started, she'd have a hard time stoppin' on account'a bein' so tired and secretly very, very scared.

Layin' down on the wooden floor—it looked like sealed walnut, or maybe hickory—she slid back under the flightpanel and gazed up at Tilden's handiwork. There was the cylindrical fluctuator she'd gone to such pains to find, plugged in snugly between the leveler connectors. Such a small part to rely on. It didn't even look like it belonged…it was just *supposed* to go there. Why? The fluctuator regulated the amount'a power the levelers demanded'a the engine, which kept it from floodin'…but who said it was supposed to go *there*? Now that Po thought about it, it didn't make a whole lot'a sense.

And airship engineerin' was all about good sense. Math and a head for figures helped, but Da had always said a mechanic's gut was his most valuable tool. Once you knew enough about airships, how they lived and breathed, you could feel when somethin' was off. Like a doctor, determinin' a diagnosis after listenin' to a person's heart.

Somethin' about *Lady Isabelle* and that tricksome little fluctuator just felt off to Po, and that made her realize somethin' important. Somethin' she'd already known, that had been driftin' the peripheral'a her mind.

She knew enough about airships to be gettin' on with; stayin' at The Owl from today forward would be nothin' but formality. When she put a stethoscope to her own heartbeat to listen to what she really felt, she realized a part'a her had felt like if she honored Da's wishes for her to stay in school, it would bring him back. It wouldn't, no more than choosin' to save *Trimble and Sons* with Gus and

Tilden would keep him away. If she chose to believe he was comin' home at all, then she chose to believe he would do it no matter what. That was how hope worked.

Po reached, and bracin' herself with a scrunched-up face, yanked out the fluctuator and sat it on her stomach. In a flurry'a motion, she grabbed either'a the connectors and jerry-rigged them together. Then she lay still, starin' at what she'd done, feelin' triumphant and shocked both at once. After a moment, she scooted out from under the panel, and pinnin' the warm fluctuator under her arm, sat in the pilot's bucket-like leather seat. Hookin' the toes'a her boots under the leveler rod, she fired up the engine and eased the rod up towards her knees.

The Bylink 12-Twelve purred like a happy, sleepy kitten. Po threw her hands over her head—droppin' the fluctator in the process—and screamed.

Whether it was the scream or the engine hummin' that drew them, Gus, Tilden, and Mr. Blackwood rushed into the workshop one after the other. Tilden's jaw went slack, but grumpy Gus was a little less reserved. He gave a leap like a theatre dancer and pumped his fists as Uriah Blackwood curiously came to stand by *Lady Isabelle's* wing, his hands folded into the sleeves'a his black coat. Still grinnin', Po tuned down the engine. Then she opened the canopy window and stood in the pilot's chair.

"Whadya think?" she called. "I bet you've never heard anythin' so sweet! She could sing a baby to sleep! Ain't she just sparklin'?"

"Well, yes, though it's hard to tell in this light, truth be told," Mr. Blackwood said earnestly, but then he gave one'a his bubblin' laughs and bowed to her so she felt like a proper queen, standin' with one'a her dirty boots propped on the flight panel, her hands on her hips and her braid pinned 'round her head like a crown. Blackwood moved closer, timid and excited in sudden, jerky bursts. "I must confess

I'm surprised! Quite! With all the strife the other mechanics in the district gave me…would you believe some of them called my Isabelle a...what's the word, ah, a *junker*?"

It would'a been dishonest'a Po to say *no*, so she just smiled, and Blackwood laughed again. He offered her a bejeweled hand. She skipped down outta the cockpit, landin' between her two brothers as they moved up to surround her. Tilden slapped her on the back, Gus tugged her braid fondly, and she hugged them both, one arm for each. It wasn't Po's happiest memory ever, but it definitely topped any in her recent memory. She felt like they'd started somethin' with this small step, like they'd found a way to repel the darkness in the warm thrum'a *Lady Isabelle* and the relief'a seein' Gus really smile again. They'd planted a seed'a hope and watered it, and for the first time in a long time, enough light was bein' let in for it to really start to grow.

There was just one thing left for Po to do. It was hard to believe it would be the hardest thing she had done yet today.

V

Po could'a used some rain. Somethin'—anythin'—
to fill the silence in Headmaster Eldritch's waitin' room.

Hands folded under her legs, she gazed around in
awe. She really hoped this wasn't where Da's hard-earned
tuition money was goin', but she didn't suppose Eldritch
paid for it all outta pocket. Marble floors splashed the
light'a the photon chandelier onto the wallpapered walls,
leather couches, and hangin' green plants. A loomin'
portrait'a the headmaster that had to be nearly life-size
hung over the stone fireplace to Po's right, while to her left,
a wooden globe'a Honora stood on spindly legs, throwin'
its animal-like shadow across her lap. Everythin' about the
room just felt *big*; maybe because in this moment, she felt
so small.

Muted voices mumbled on the other side'a the twin
oak doors to Eldritch's study. Apart from the grey-haired
Miss Maple, who Po could barely see over the tall counter
hedgin' her into her workspace, there was no one else
around. Everyone would be in class…or *should* be,
anyways. There was no doubt a fair number'a students was
skivin' to visit the festival planetside. Po could'a told them
all about it, seein' as she'd been stalled in parade traffic for
a good three hours before finally catchin' a bus-ship back to
Atlas.

After Blackwood had settled his bill and flown
Lady Isabelle out (Po had held her breath the whole time.
Wouldn't it just have figured, him crashin' the Chimera
before he even left the shop?), Po and her brothers had sent
a log to Mum to tell her the good news. She hadn't looked
surprised in the least, though she did watch Po's face

closely while Gus and Tilden talked over top'a each other, and Po could tell she knew more had been decided than just the success'a their shop. She hadn't said anythin', just smiled so her eyes crinkled and told them all she was proud, and from Frances Trimble, that was permission enough.

Po had been packin' up her things and brushin' out her frazzled braid when Gus and Tilden had cornered her with near identical grins. Gus held somethin' behind his back—a million shields, or at least that's what his giddy grin suggested.

"We owe you for this one, Po," Tilden had said, which was about as close to admittin' he'd been wrong as Tilden ever came. He shuffled his feet. "You saved our necks."

After tryin' for a minute, Po gave up on not lookin' so pleased with herself and beamed. "Well, just you remember next time you want to go temptin' Ubber—"

Then Gus pulled out their present, and Po's chin tried to touch her toes. In his dirty hands was a beautiful book...a stained book, with frayed edges and dog-eared corners, its green leather cracked and supple. Immediately, she grabbed it, opened it wide, and stuck her nose deep into the pages, breathin' in the smell'a Da. *The Silver Shrew*. He used to read it to them all the time, but Po hadn't seen it since he'd left. Now it occurred to her that Gus and Tilden in all their childish tantrum-throwin' might'a hid it outta spite, puttin' it away like they'd put away the pictures'a him, put away all their hurt.

"You hold this family together, you know," Gus said, hesitantly touchin' the book, like he was askin' its forgiveness.

"Naw," Po had said as she'd brushed a finger over the silhouette'a the shrew etched into the tired leather. "I just won't let anyone break it apart."

Po perked up, snappin' back to the present. The muffled voices in the headmaster's office had trailed off. Suddenly, the golden curlicue handle twisted on one'a Eldritch's doors. Her heart and stomach leaped together as the door opened and Reece Sheppard, the Grand Duke's son himself, slipped out. She'd just seen him in class two days ago, but, well…Reece was the kind'a unfussy handsome that always took her pleasantly by surprise. She found herself bitin' back a grin.

Reece smiled at Miss Maple as she eyed him over the tops'a her spectacles. She held out an age-spotted hand, and he passed her a note. Prolly an invoice for a disciplinary fine his parents would be expected to pay with his next month's tuition. Po couldn't see the figure, but she shuddered all the same.

Miss Maple held the note at arm's length and stared narrowly down her nose at it. "Good gracious, Mr. Sheppard. I don't believe I've ever seen such a fee."

"That's mine and Gideon Creed's rolled into one," Reece explained, and tried to point to a line on the note as if Miss Maple wasn't readin' it right.

Miss Maple swatted his hand away. "Volunteering your parents' money again, I see. Should I send them a log?"

"If you want."

"Do they know you were caught skipping class?"

"Not yet. Are you going to tell them?"

The secretary studied Reece's expression—honest, curious, and maybe just a little cheeky—and smiled thinly. "I suspect they would hardly be surprised if I did. No, I'll leave that up to you. And I dare say this fine will speak for itself once it's posted."

Reece made a face, but quickly recovered his good humor. He gave Miss Maple a nod, readjusted the satchel slung over his shoulder, and backed towards the door. Po had to stand and take a quick step to one side lest she be run over. Even then, Reece's heel still bumped her toe, and he stumbled a bit, lookin' at her.

"Oh, hey," he said, surprised, "sorry."

He ducked out the before Po could more than blush and smile. Rats! She hardly ever got the chance to talk to Reece on account'a them runnin' in such different circles, and after today, she wouldn't even have those few chances. For all she knew, this could be the last time she ever saw Reece Sheppard. She studied the back'a his messy brown head as he disappeared down the corridor, just in case. It was a view that hadn't changed much in the three years she'd snuck glances at it in class, but she'd miss it all the same. It always made her feel warm and melted inside, like one'a Mum's gooey biscuits.

"Miss Trimble," Miss Maple prompted. "Headmaster Eldritch is waiting."

Drawin' up her shoulders with a deep breath, Po said a silent goodbye to the back'a Reece's head and marched toward the headmaster's imposin' doors. Miss Maple gave her an A-class stink eye as she passed, but after all she'd been through today and yesterday, she refused to be bullied. Her decision was made, and even if no one else in the world agreed, Po knew in the deepest part'a her that it was right. She had to hold onto that belief with both hands, not lettin' anyone shake her loose, no matter how dumb they made her feel. It was a lot easier said than done, but the more Po preached to herself, the braver she felt about steppin' into Eldritch's office and closin' the door at her back.

She was alone with the headmaster like she'd never been before. The office was tunnel-like, a long and narrow walk'a scarlet carpet deliverin' visitors to the headmaster's claw-footed desk, which stood in the light of a huge round window overlookin' the campus green. Eldritch was a hazy shape set against that light, standin' with his back to Po, his spidery hands clasped behind his back.

Feelin' tiny but determined, Po approached the desk, passin' under a tiered photon chandelier that buzzed like insect whispers. She chanced a curious look around. From the carpeted floor to the domed ceilin', the office's walls were nothin' but orderly shelves'a books and files. There were no picture frames'a family, no keepsakes from a past life. It was like the headmaster wanted students to think he'd always been headmaster, and that's all he ever would be.

Headmaster Eldritch turned just as Po slipped onto the plain wooden stool before the desk. Dressed in a three-piece black suit with a black cravat and pocket hanky, he looked ready for a funeral. But he smiled.

"Ah, Miss Trimble," he greeted in that breathy voice he had. He flipped the tails'a his coat out as he settled into his chair and ran his hands just once over his slicked-back hair. "A pleasure to see you here. Tutor Agnes has been singing your praises for a year now." His beady eyes roved her without so much as a twinkle. "Might I enquire as to the reason for your visit?"

Po pressed her fidgetin' hands together between her knees. "I'm here to quit The Owl." She sounded so matter-o'-fact, impressively relaxed. She blamed it on all'a this feelin' surreal—especially with the merry birdsong comin' through the office window. The sun split through two oak branches out on the green, beamin' into her eyes.

Eldritch's thin eyebrows furrowed over his long nose; the effect was not becoming. Leanin' back in his chair, he steepled his hands together, fingertips perfectly aligned, and studied her as she squirmed.

"So," Po continued when he went on starin', "whatever papers you need me to sign, I'll just do that now. And I want you to know, it's not that I don't appreciate everythin' The Owl is, it's just—"

"Has the financial burden become too much for your family?" Eldritch interrupted, and the way he looked over his fingers at her, with his dark eyes gleamin' thoughtfully, made Po feel like she was talkin' to some kind'a head doctor who was gonna try to prescribe her somethin' for her craziness. But she wasn't crazy, and she didn't appreciate the presumption that her family was too poor to manage her school bills…even if it was mostly true. She dusted off the lap'a her jumpsuit and raised her chin.

"I want to be an airship mechanic. The way I see it, I can be, right now, in my brothers' shop."

Eldritch tipped his head like a curious bird and smiled like he thought she was tryin' to be cute. "That would be a mistake, Miss Trimble. And I'll tell you why," he added, raisin' a finger to forestall her as she opened her mouth, "if you'll but listen." He stood—which was a long process, on account'a him bein' so tall; his legs just kept on comin'. Po craned her neck to watch him as he slid out from behind his desk, straightened his jacket, and started pacin' circles around her. The way he walked—almost glidin' more than takin' actual steps—unnerved her. He was so quiet. She could imagine many a student sittin' right where she was and cavin' to that dark gaze before a proper interrogation could even begin.

"You are a Fourteen, yes? From what Tutor Agnes tells me, you have already surpassed many of the Eighteens with twice the opportunity and half the disadvantages as you." Eldritch's tone was conversational, but his words sounded rehearsed…which made Po feel all the stupider for not knowin' how to reply. He stepped over her uncomfortable pause with a gracious bow'a his head, like she ought'a be thankin' him for his manners. "Now, say you do leave The Academy. In one year, you might still be satisfied with the monotony of waking up every day with nothing to do but *get by*. But in two years, you will begin to get restless. In three years, once your regret catches up to you, it will be too late for you to change your mind. And in four years, when all your would-be fellow graduates take their Career Aptitude tests and go on to do great things, forgetting your name, and that you were ever one of them…well, Miss Trimble, I fear that your own stagnancy might very well undo you."

Eldritch stopped before Po, lookin' down at her with grave sympathy. Po's lip quivered. Then she burst out laughin', coverin' her mouth with her hands. In truth, she'd only understood half'a what he'd said, but she got the gist. He was tryin' to scare her outta quittin' school. If only he knew. In all her dallyin' over a decision, Po had never once been scared she'd ruin her own life. Life was what you made it, and she could be happy either way, with The Owl, without The Owl. She'd simply wanted the choice to be *right*. Now that she knew for certain it was, she wasn't scared at all. Just ready to begin.

"I'm sorry, Headmaster," she apologized through her last few giggles. "It's just…well, last night I was tryin' to fix an airship. A Chimera." She waited for that to register with the headmaster, but Eldritch just quirked an eyebrow and perched on the edge'a his desk. So Po continued, "Anyways, I was so sure there was somethin' wrong with the ship—not that there wasn't, I mean, it was a *Chimera*, after all—but it kept me from lookin' at the smaller parts. The big picture is important, but you don't really appreciate it until you get your nose up close to the little details and then pull back. I suppose I'll get to the big picture eventually, and you know, maybe I *will* be a lil' sorry I never finished at The Owl. But right now, I got a chance to do somethin' that really makes me happy and help my family. And right now is awfully important too."

After all that, Headmaster Eldritch just looked at

her. He very slowly crossed his arms over his chest and tapped a finger thoughtfully against his wrinkled lips. "You are making a mistake, Miss Trimble," he said at length, makin' Po blink. "I cannot say it any plainer. A few years' experience in a Westerner shop is nothing compared to having a hard-earned diploma behind your name."

Grimacin', Po stood. Who would'a thought the hardest part'a quittin' would be convincin' the headmaster himself to let her do it? Gus and Tilden were gonna love that. "Sorry, Sir, but I gotta stick with my gut on this one, you know?"

"The school would be prepared to offer you a small stipend to stay on as a student," Eldritch said right over top'a her, still tappin' his lips.

A stipend. Po tugged her braid, wonderin' if that meant what she thought it meant. "You wanna bribe me to stay a student?"

"Bribe you?" Eldritch laughed. He clasped his hands together. "No, no. *Encourage* you. How can I say this delicately? Many of the students at The Aurelian Academy make it into the school on the merits of their parents' wallets alone. But you, Ms. Trimble, are one of the few true geniuses we have to our name. I would be most displeased to lose you."

"So you want me to stay…because I'm smart." Po frowned and fought the urge to stamp her hands on her hips like Mum would'a done. "And I suppose that looks awfully good on paper, huh?"

Displeasure came across Eldritch's face in a flash'a shadow, like a cloud had suddenly rolled across the sky. But out the window, the birds were still chirpin' and the swayin' trees looked gilded in the sunlight. It was just the headmaster's office that suddenly felt chilly and still, as if a vacuum had opened up with Eldritch at its mouth.

"Yes," he said, leanin' forward like he had a secret.

"For there is no other reason we would have you, Miss Trimble. So stay, or throw away your future. I will make no more offers."

For the briefest'a seconds, Po hesitated. Not because what he was sayin' was at all temptin', but because she knew this was a threshold, and she was about to pull a door shut for good. It was a dauntin' feelin'. But nowhere near as dauntin' as the thought'a owin' this man *any* favors. She shivered. "It's just as well," she said meekly. "I wouldn't wanna have to turn any more down."

Eldritch's smile stretched, taut. He spun, the tails'a his coat flyin', and swept around his desk to rummage through a small bin'a files. "Indeed," he murmured, almost to himself. "Indeed you wouldn't. Ah." He brandished a slip'a parchment between two'a his fingers, read it over briefly, and then signed it with a black quill. "There. Give this to Miss Maple. She'll be in touch with your mother and arrange for your dormitory to be cleaned and the remainder of your semester's allowances refunded."

Po took the parchment in her hands carefully, her eyes blurrin' at all the cramped little addendums and details. Her four wonderful years at The Owl, summed up in a few paragraphs she'd never even read. She felt a tug'a bittersweet sadness, and looked up.

Outside the headmaster's window, life at The Owl went on without missin' a step. Students punted in the lake or picnicked on blankets on the green with schoolbooks and datascopes spread around them like a feast. A flock'a blue swans cut through the cloud'a steam risin' over the bell tower'a from the Iron Horse. Po hoisted up her bag on her shoulder, and feelin' the pleasant weight'a *The Silver Shrew* like an anchor in its belly, smiled. She would miss this place, but she suspected she'd be back before long. Tutor Agnes was always hirin' out city help, and the school's bus-ships wouldn't fix themselves, though maybe with a little time and a lot'a love, Po could teach them to.

"Good luck, Miss Trimble," Eldritch said airily as she turned to go. She looked back, ready to thank him politely like Da would have her do, but his attention was already elsewhere, on a new file for a new student, like Po stayin' or goin' didn't matter after all. She wanted to stomp her way out, just to be heard. But in honor'a Da, she said crisply, "Thank you, Headmaster. You have a good day, now," and topped it off with a cheerful skip as she left his office for good.

Made in the USA
Lexington, KY
01 June 2016